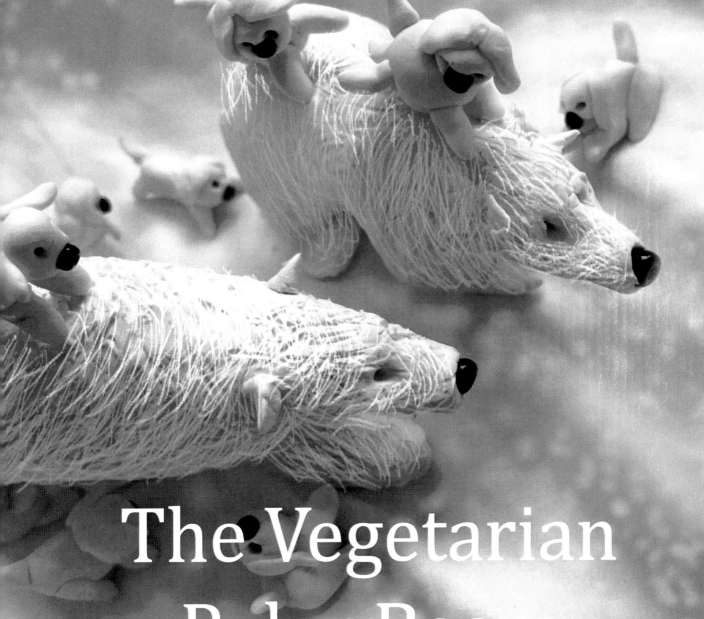

The Vegetarian
Polar Bears

G C PAGE

Why carrots all around me??
I am Oneo.
I'm guarding this hillside!!!
Vegetable eating varmints
are out there.

I live in the Village of MeCold.
It is located behind the Great
Bear Sleeping Sand Dune.

I have lived through the Great
Snowstorm and then the
Invasion of the Snow Puppies.
Things were calm around
here for awhile but then an
unbelievable event occurred.
I'll tell you about it!!!

We kids were having great fun on the snowy and sunny days. The Snow Fairy was kind to us and gave us just enough snow and wonderfully cold weather.

We had plenty of snow boulders and plenty of room to pass them around. So, we exercised and had fun, fun, and more fun!!!

Trunks, a giant cold one, had a
reunion of his buddies from
The Great Snowstorm. All were
pleasingly healthy and cheerful. I had
another chance to stand up on his arm.

We were very fortunate to survive The
Great Snowstorm!!

Trunks and the Grippers were the true
heroes during that storm!!

Top Hat, who was born after The Great Snowstorm, was lecturing again about the weather, its highs and lows, over and over again, until everyone was bored!!

The Elders were talking about
what was new, what was old,
what did happen, and what
might happen.

Soon, as the sun began to set,
they were all tired and prepared
for sleep.

They slept very soundly. Before the sun rose, something horrible had happened. Once the morning light illuminated the scene the kids were laughing, but the elders were crying !!!!

I could not stop laughing seeing
Pede without a nose. And, then I
saw Ruffy laughing and without
a nose!!

Ha, ha, haa, haaa they all roared!!

Flake was laughing at
Carlott's new haircut. Carlott
was laughing at Flake's
plain face.
Ha, ha, haaaa!!!!

Fred was laughing at
Snowballs face.
Snowballs laughed!!!
"You funny lookin' !!!!"
Fred replied, "No! You
funny looking!!!"

I quit laughing when I saw Five Dip. He seemed to be very concerned. "I can't breathe!!" he gasped!!

The Icelandic Sisters were crying.
"What are we to do, we can't be seen."
They sobbed, "We have to hide, but
there is nowhere to hide our faces."

Then they shook in sadness and wept,
"The beauty pageant is in two weeks,
we need help! Hellppp!!!"

The Gripper did not look so strong without a nose. Trunks had huge bites out of his huge nose!! "What bit me??" Trunks asked. "Almost everyone lost their noses."

"We look so plain" Goldie wispered to Iceman. "We are not ourselves," Iceman replied!!!

"Where did our noses go??" They wondered.

Where did
the noses
go???

Fred found
the answers
sleeping next
to frozen
carrot juice!!!

When Fred told Doc Coldman. Doc feared the Polar Bears were vegetarian. "We have to rid of these Bears, or our noses will never be safe."

Doc asked Top Hat and Fred to bring back the Snow Puppies.

Fred and Top Hat traveled to Snow Puppy Park and started rolling the snow boulders. The Snow Puppies followed, dancing and prancing, rolling and strolling, playing and straying until they reached the sleeping Vegetarian Polar Bears.

The Vegetarian Polar Bears woke when the Snow Puppies pawed and clawed, snuggled and rolled, crawled and climbed all over them.

Although fearless, the Bears woke from a dream to a scarry idea!!!
"Are these all our Snow Cubs?"
"How can we feed them, teach them, and pay for their educations??"

"Run!!" And they began to run out of the Village with the Snow Puppies close behind!!

The Snow Puppies,
dancing and prancing,
rolling and strolling,
playing and straying
chased the
Vegetarian Polar Bears
out of the Village of
MeCold and out of the
County of WeCold.

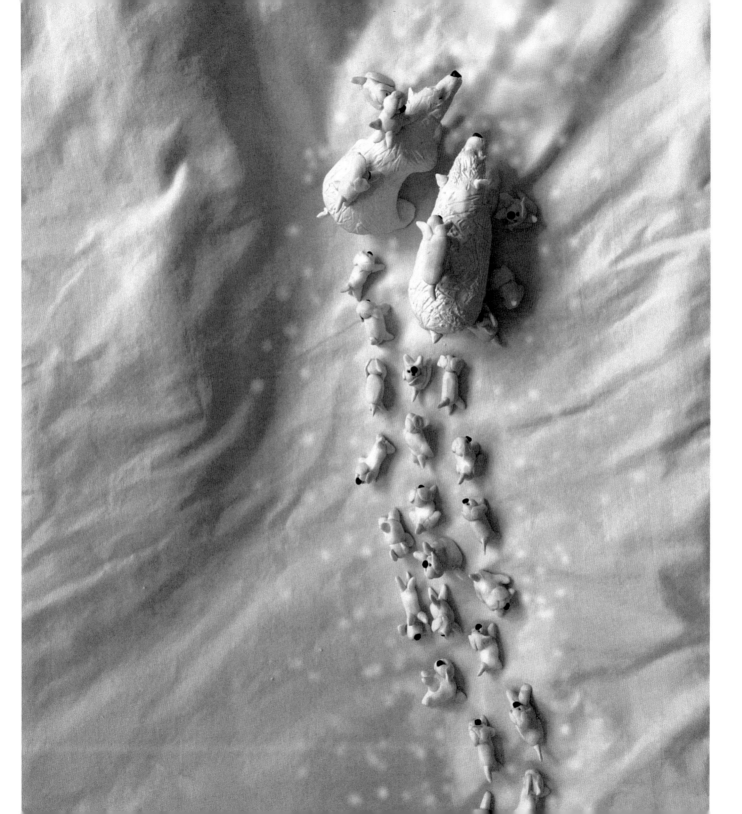

"We need new noses!!!" Doc Coldman cried. "We need to send a message to the Vegetable Specialist in MeSick."

The Gripper placed the message in a snowball while Trunks held the ends of the slingshot.

Trunks had removed
his hat for a clearer
shot.

The Gripper stretched
and stretched the
bands until he could
not pull any further.
The message had a
long distance to go!!!

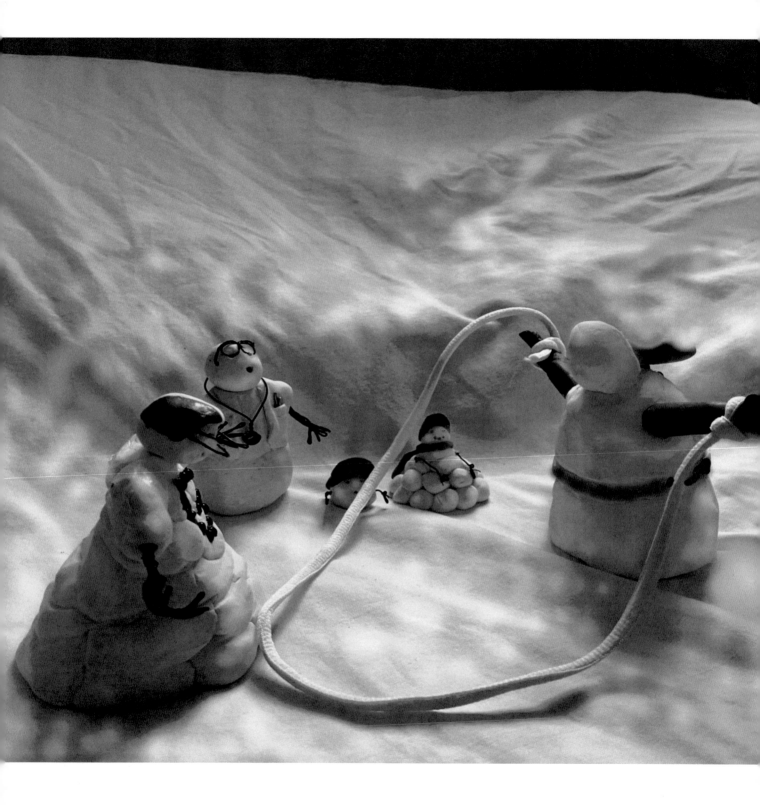

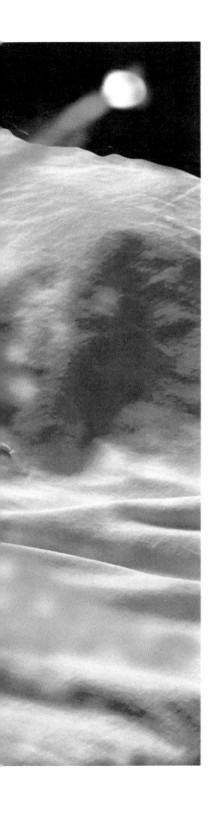

The snowball was launched, and it flew high past the Village of MeCold, over the Lake of Crystals, over the Town of Beulah, over the County of WeCold and landed next to Dr. Carsel and Dr. Pumpkinhead in the Village of MeSick.

Dr. Pumpkinhead and Dr. Carsel were known throughout the State of Frigid as Vegetable Specialists and Surgeons. Dr. Carsel read the message to Dr. Pumpkinhead!!

"We need help!!! Vegetarian Polar Bears ate most of our noses........."

Dr. Pumpkinhead had a daymare while standing there. The Vegetarian Polar Bears were chasing him!!!!

A long line of Snow Puppies were riding and chasing the polar bears.

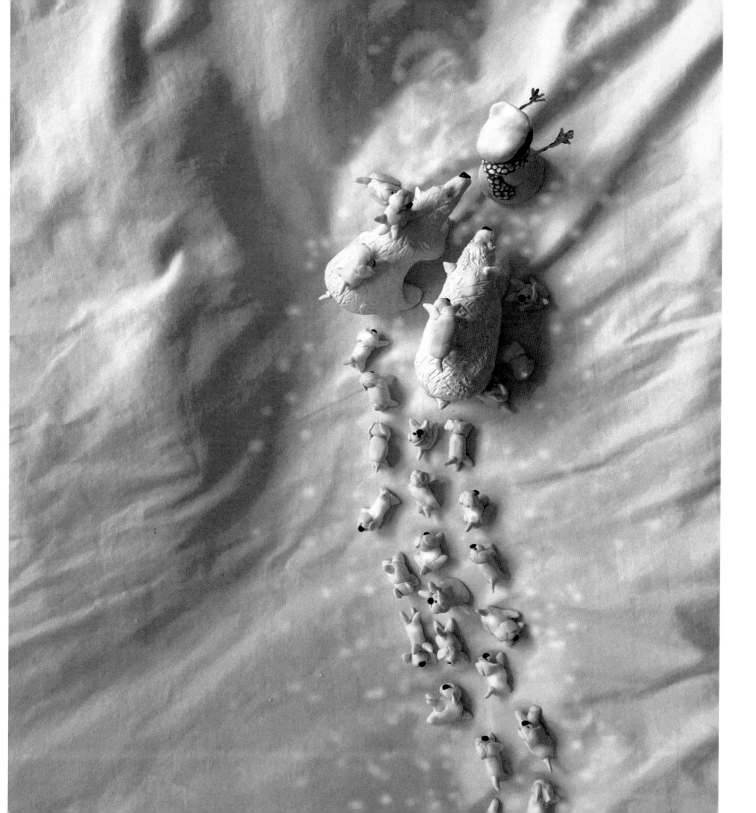

The Vegetarian Polar Bears were curiously
sniffing him and were drooling.

They were licking and chomping and
showing their teeth!!!!

They were ready to take a
bite out of his head when
Dr. Carsel continued with
the unfinished message
in the letter..........

.........The Vegetarian Polar Bears were chased away. No worry!! They are a long, long way from the Village of MeCold."

Pumpkinhead was relieved and continued to fill the vegetable sled for the long trip.

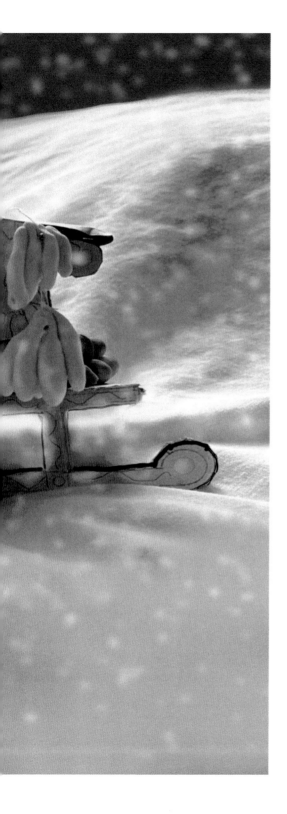

The two walked off pulling their sled toward the Village of MeCold. They crossed the sugar maple forests and entered into the County of WeCold. They crossed the frozen Lake of Crystals and then entered the Village.

The noseless cheered as Dr. Pumpkinhead and Dr. Carsel arrived that morning in MeCold. The Cold Ones were relieved. Soon their faces would be normal.

Dr. Carsel and Dr. Pumpkinhead spent the morning carving the carrots, and then the Cold Ones lined up one by one until all of them had their operations.

By the end of the day, the Cold Ones had new noses. They all looked great, refreshed and whole again.

They spent hours just looking at each other. They were so happy, they announced "let's celebrate, yes, let's celebrate!!!"

The celebration lasted two days. All the Village of MeCold Cold Ones were invited along with the Snow Puppies, Dr. Pumpkinhead and Dr. Carsel.

The Cold Ones were jitterbugging. The old and young were dancing. The Snow Puppies were wiggling, and the kids were giggling. All were dancing and prancing, rolling and strolling all night long!!!

Not everyone was
invited to the celebration.
Some looked on from afar,
hungry and lonely!!!

THE HAPPY ENDING !!!

Is your nose still there?

Copyright 2023
by Gregory Charles Page

ORANGE EXPRESSION LLC

Dr. Carsel   Dr. Pumpkinhead

Pa   Auntie   Ma

Coalena   Carlotta   Freda   Goldie

The Cold Ones and Visitors of the Village of MeCold

Fred   Flake   Top Hat

The Icelandic Sisters

Gripper   Iceman   Doc Coldman

Oneo   Pede   Snowballs   Carlott   Five Dip   Ruffy

Trunks

Made in the USA
Las Vegas, NV
02 August 2023

75305586R10048